DISNEY

Anna & Elsa

The Arendelle Cup

To JoAnne Johnson,
auntie, confidante, and friend
—E.D.

randomhousekids.com

ISBN 978-0-7364-3437-9 (hardcover) — ISBN 978-0-7364-8202-8 (lib. bdg.)

Printed in the United States of America

10 9 8 7 6 5 4 3 2 1

Anna & Elsa

The Arendelle Cup

By Erica David

Illustrated by Bill Robinson,
Manuela Razzi, Francesco Legramandi,
and Gabriella Matta

Random House New York

Chapter 1

"Mush, Sven! Mush!" Elsa shouted. She and Anna were riding side by side in a racing sled. Sven the reindeer pulled them across the snowy fields outside Arendelle. The winter wind whipped through their hair and roared in their ears.

Elsa leaned forward, gripping the reins. She guided Sven through huge dunes of snow.

"All this racing is making me hungry!" Anna said.

"We're almost there!" Elsa replied. She tapped Sven gently with the reins. The reindeer picked up speed. He raced over the frosty field, towing the bright red sled as quickly as he could. The sled sped silently on its runners.

"Look, there's Kristoff!" Elsa said.

Kristoff was standing a couple hundred feet away, holding a pocket watch. He was timing Anna and Elsa. From a distance he looked tiny. But as the sled drew closer, he grew larger.

"Yip, yip!" Elsa called to Sven. The reindeer's ears flattened as he listened to Elsa's command. They were approaching

the final stretch. It was time for Sven to sprint. His large hooves drummed swiftly against the ground.

The sled moved so fast, Elsa felt like she was flying.

"Woo-hoo!" Anna shouted.

The finish line was in sight. Kristoff waved his arms above his head encouragingly.

"Whoa!" Elsa said, pulling back on the reins. Sven understood that it was time to slow down. But he was running too fast! Momentum carried him forward.

"Slow down, Sven!" Anna told him.

The sled barreled downhill toward Kristoff at an alarming speed. "Uh, now might be a good time to stop!" he shouted.

Sven dug his hooves into the snow. He tried to stop, but he was too close to Kristoff! The reindeer began to slide on the icy ground.

At the last moment, Kristoff dived out of the way. Elsa pulled hard on the reins. The sled skidded to the side, throwing up a sheet of snow. The snow whooshed through the air, covering Kristoff from head to toe.

"Whoa!" Elsa said again as Sven found his footing. Finally, the sled came to a complete stop.

Anna threw her arms in the air. "That was some finish!"

"I'll say!" Elsa replied.

"What's our time?" Anna asked.

Kristoff shook the snow from his clothes and looked at the watch. "Eight minutes and twenty-seven seconds," he answered.

"Not too shabby," Anna said proudly.

"Do you think it's fast enough?" Elsa asked, worried. She and Anna were practicing for the Arendelle Cup, a famous sled race. Every year, teams came from all over the world to compete. Now that the castle gates were open, Anna and Elsa could finally participate.

"Sure it's fast enough," Anna said. "After all, this race is more about endurance."

Elsa realized that Anna was right. The Arendelle Cup was a long race. It covered one hundred fifty miles and took three days. Each two-person team had to travel fifty miles a day!

"Well, lucky for you, Sven is one hearty reindeer," Kristoff said.

"You've got that right," Anna agreed, patting Sven gently. "Thank you for letting him pull our sled, Kristoff."

"You're welcome," he replied.

"I think we're the only team with a reindeer this year," Elsa told him. Each team used different animals to pull its sled. Some used horses, while others used sled dogs.

"I'm just glad Sven will have the chance to represent Arendelle," Kristoff said, smiling.

"I'm sure he'll make you proud," Elsa said.

"He'd better, because this whole fastest-reindeer-in-the-kingdom thing is starting to go to his head," Kristoff responded.

The reindeer nickered softly in protest.

"How?" Anna asked.

"I'm too fast for ice harvesting," Kristoff answered in his Sven voice.

"Sven, are you saying the ice harvesters can't keep up?" Anna teased playfully.

"Of course not!" Kristoff replied in his normal voice. "We harvesters have no trouble keeping up with a reindeer."

"Let's just hope the other teams do," Elsa said.

The sisters climbed out of the sled and unhitched Sven. Kristoff gave the reindeer a carrot. The sun was just beginning to set behind the snow dunes.

"Look at the time, Anna. We should probably head back to the castle," Elsa pointed out.

"You're right," Anna said. "Our guests will be arriving soon."

Anna and Elsa were hosting a welcome party for the Arendelle Cup teams. Most of them had traveled from far away. The girls couldn't wait to greet them. But they were nervous, too. The other teams had a lot of experience. Team Arendelle was in for some stiff competition.

Chapter 2

Later, the castle ballroom hummed with polite conversation. The racing teams had arrived! All of Arendelle had gathered to welcome the visitors. Everyone was eating and chatting pleasantly. Elsa and Anna moved through the crowd, shaking hands with their honored guests.

"Welcome to Arendelle!" Elsa greeted the team from Eldora. She remembered her first visit to the desert kingdom. She and Anna had mistakenly thought that the country was trapped in eternal summer! But that wasn't the case: Eldora simply had hot weather year-round.

The Eldoran team was made up of cousins named Nina and Naia. They wore bright dresses the color of saffron and paprika—spices that the kingdom was known for.

"Pleased to meet you," said Naia. She and Nina curtsied graciously.

"Nice to meet you, too," Anna told them.

"We hope you're enjoying Arendelle so far," Elsa said.

Nina and Naia exchanged a smile.

"It's wonderful!" Nina exclaimed. "Arendelle's climate is so different from Eldora's."

"With your weather, you have all kinds of plants we've never seen!" Naia chimed in. She showed Anna and Elsa a leather-bound book. "We've been drawing them

in our plant journal. We love studying plants."

Elsa looked through the journal's pages. There were detailed drawings of all sorts of plants from Eldora and around the world.

Elsa furrowed her brow in thought. There was no snow in Eldora. In fact, the country got all of its ice from Arendelle. If the people of Eldora were used to warm weather, how would they fare in a snow race?

As if reading Elsa's mind, Anna asked, "How did you practice for the race without snow?"

"Most of the year we race our horses on

sand," Nina explained. "Then we spend a month or two in a snowy place."

"That's the toughest part of training," Naia said. "Snow makes me want to play, not practice."

"I know the feeling," Anna replied.

"Did someone say snow?" cried a familiar voice.

Olaf bounced through the crowd. He spotted Nina and Naia and hurried over to meet them.

"Hello! Your clothes remind me of summer!" Olaf exclaimed. "Are you from Eldora?" He had visited Eldora with Anna and Elsa.

"You've been to our kingdom?" Nina asked him.

"Yes! It's so hot and bright and summery! I love summer!" Olaf said.

"I didn't think our climate would be so popular with a snowman," Nina said.

"Just *this* snowman," Elsa said with a smile.

Olaf bowed deeply to Naia and Nina. "Please tell the Summer Queen hello!"

"The Summer Queen?" Nina asked, confused.

Olaf had once thought that Eldora's queen had powers like Elsa's—except that she could control fire and heat. It turned out that she didn't have any powers, but Olaf still called her the Summer Queen.

"He means Queen Marisol," Elsa explained.

"Oh," Nina said, nodding. "Certainly. We'll tell the queen you said hello."

Anna and Elsa wished Nina and Naia good luck. They turned back to the crowded ballroom to greet the other visitors. Elsa noticed the team from Chatho standing next to a tray of desserts.

"I'm Queen Elsa of Arendelle," she introduced herself. "This is my sister, Princess Anna."

The team nodded, bowing slightly in a gesture of respect.

"Of course, you're our hosts. My name is Tashi, and this is my friend Tenzin," the girl said. She gave Anna and Elsa a friendly smile. Her shoulder-length, dark hair was fastened in a neat barrette. She wore a long red robe trimmed in gold.

Tashi was the same height as Anna. But Tenzin was nearly a foot taller. He had short, dark hair and soft brown eyes. He wore a loose-fitting tunic belted with a ceremonial sword strapped to his waist.

"A pleasure to meet you," Tenzin told them. "We bring a gift from Queen Colisa."

Tenzin drew a small silk pouch from his pocket and handed it to Tashi. She opened the pouch and took out a tiny figurine.

Elsa gasped in delight. It was a statue of a Chathan sloth.

"It's wonderful," Anna said. Tashi set the figurine in Anna's palm. It was beautifully carved from jade. The surface sparkled a brilliant shade of green.

"The queen sends her regards," Tenzin said. "She had this carved by two of Chatho's finest sculptors."

"Who?" Elsa asked curiously.

Tenzin and Tashi exchanged a smile.

"Us," Tashi replied. She reached into the pocket of her robe and took out a small chisel. "When we're not racing yaks, Tenzin and I love to sculpt."

"That's amazing!" Anna said. Chatho was famous for its art.

"When do you have time to race?" asked Elsa. "It looks like this took forever to make."

"We make time for the things we love to do," Tenzin answered.

Elsa thanked Team Chatho heartily, and Anna gave them a polite bow.

At the other end of the ballroom, a group of musicians struck up a tune. At once the villagers and guests found partners to dance with. Two determined young men walked purposefully across the room toward Anna and Elsa. They stopped in front of the girls and bowed deeply.

"Your Majesty," said the shorter of the two men. He was blond and had a huge handlebar mustache. The hair above his lip flapped gently as he spoke. "I am Leopold von Amstel of Weselton. May I have this dance?"

Before Elsa could reply, Leopold swept her into a waltz. She looked over her shoulder for sympathy from Anna, but she, too, had a partner. The taller of the two men, Lutz, had whisked her onto the dance floor.

"Uh, hello," Elsa said, surprised. She held the skirt of her gown to keep it out of the way. The men of Weselton were spirited dancers. She remembered the Duke of Weselton's fancy footwork at her coronation.

"I would like to thank Your Majesty for inviting us to be in this year's Arendelle Cup," Leopold said. "I know relations between our kingdoms haven't been the best."

Arendelle had stopped trading with Weselton after Elsa became queen. The

Duke of Weselton's greed had put an end to their partnership. But Elsa thought it would be sporting to allow Weselton to participate in the race.

"Well, I hope we can be friends," Elsa responded.

"Friends?" asked Leopold with a smirk. "I'll leave that for you to decide. You might not want to be friends after Lutz and I beat you."

"Oh, you're going to beat us?" Elsa challenged.

"It's a fact. We're the best sledding team in the world. Our mules are un-paralleled," he explained, puffing his chest. "Surely you don't think you and

your sister can win when you've never raced before?"

"Time will tell," Elsa said politely. "But we've practiced and worked hard."

Leopold laughed, clearly unimpressed. "Well, just don't expect us to let you win," he scoffed. Elsa stopped dancing and stepped away from him.

"Thank you for the dance," she told him firmly.

Leopold clicked his heels together. He gave Elsa a mocking bow and signaled to his teammate. Lutz inclined his head politely to Anna before walking off with Leopold.

Anna noticed the annoyed look on

Elsa's face. She hurried over to her sister.

"What happened?" Anna asked.

"Was your dance partner as rude as mine?" Elsa said.

"Didn't say a word," Anna replied with a shrug. "I take it yours did more talking."

"Most of which I didn't want to hear," Elsa responded. She told Anna about Leopold's bragging.

"I hate being underestimated," Anna said, frowning. But after a moment her smile returned.

"What is it?" Elsa asked.

"Oh, I was just thinking about how upset Team Weselton's going to be when

we prove them wrong," Anna answered.

"You're right, Anna," Elsa said. Her mood brightened. "Team Weselton will learn they're not the only contenders in the race."

"And speaking of contenders, there are the defending champions!" Anna said with excitement. She pointed to a brother-and-sister pair standing just a few feet away.

Elsa and Anna had read all about them in the village newspaper, the *Arendelle Times.* Their names were Sivoy and Suqi. They came from Tikaani, an island kingdom in the far north. Tikaani had winter weather year-round. Its residents knew everything about snow and ice. Because of the cold weather, dog sleds were the main form of transportation. Sivoy and Suqi were known for their fearless six-dog sled team. They had trained and taken care of their dogs since they were pups.

Elsa was nervous about meeting them. Team Tikaani was famous. They had won the Arendelle Cup two years in a row! Everyone was wondering if they would make it three this year.

Anna waved at Sivoy and Suqi, and the champions smiled. They walked over to say hello to Anna and Elsa.

Suqi was the first to extend her hand in greeting. "Hi there, we're—"

"We know!" Anna interrupted enthu-

siastically. "We're so excited to meet you!"

"You must be Princess Anna," Suqi said, shaking hands. "And Queen Elsa."

"We're thrilled to meet you, too," her brother, Sivoy, chimed in.

"Really? I mean, you guys are the champions!" Anna gushed. "You know *everything* about racing!"

"I wouldn't say everything," Suqi replied. "Each race is different. There's always something new to learn."

"But you look so . . . prepared!" Anna said.

Sivoy and his sister were dressed in heavy parkas and furry boots. They looked more than ready to battle the cold.

"Well, we do practice a lot," Sivoy said. "But I'm sure all the teams do."

"What about you two?" Suqi asked. "This is your first race, right? I'm sure you've practiced day and night."

"We've practiced," Elsa said. "But we don't have much experience." Even though Elsa was confident, she was worried. What if Leopold was right? She and Anna had never actually raced before.

"Are you sure about that? I hear you have *a lot* of experience with ice and snow," Sivoy told Elsa with a wink.

"I guess I do," Elsa said, blushing. She still wasn't used to talking about her powers. "We have that in common."

Suddenly, Elsa's thoughts were interrupted as a large, furry dog bounded into view. The dog leaped up and licked Elsa's face.

"Kaya! Down!" Suqi said firmly. Kaya the dog reluctantly obeyed. She sat respectfully beside her owners, her tail thumping with enthusiasm.

"Sorry about that, Your Majesty," Sivoy said. "Kaya knows she was supposed to wait in the stables with the other dogs. I guess she sneaked out and tracked us here."

"That's okay," Elsa said. "She's very friendly."

"And she likes you," Suqi explained.

Elsa knelt to scratch Kaya behind her pointed ears. Kaya was tall, with thick fur. She had a white face and belly, but her ears and the top of her coat were solid black. There was a strip of black fur across her bright blue eyes. It almost looked like she was wearing a mask. Kaya panted happily as Elsa stroked her head.

"I think you've made a new friend," Anna told her sister.

"I hope we've made friends, too," Sivoy said.

"Of course," Elsa replied, standing. "It's been such a pleasure to meet you."

Kaya stood and wagged her tail in response.

"Well, we should probably get Kaya back to the stables and turn in," Suqi said. "We have to be up bright and early tomorrow."

"Thank you so much for the welcome," Sivoy said pleasantly. "And good luck in your first race."

Anna and Elsa said their goodbyes

and watched Sivoy and Suqi leave the ballroom. Kaya padded happily after them, but not before she gave Elsa one last lick.

*

Later, after the guests had left the castle, Elsa and Anna got ready for bed.

"Are you worried about tomorrow?" Anna asked, noticing Elsa's serious expression.

Elsa paused a moment. "At first I was, but I think Sivoy and Suqi helped change that."

"How?" asked Anna.

"Between the two of us, we do know an awful lot about ice and snow," Elsa said with a smile. "I started an eternal winter—"

"—and I helped you end it," Anna said, catching on.

Elsa nodded. "Even though we haven't raced before, I think we can manage three days traveling through snow and ice," she explained.

"We do make an excellent team," Anna added.

"Exactly," Elsa replied.

Anna put her hand out for a shake. "Go, Team Arendelle!" she said.

Elsa grabbed her sister's hand to seal the deal. Now she was truly excited for the race. She couldn't wait to wake up tomorrow.

Chapter 3

The day of the race dawned clear and bright. The sky was a crisp blue. If it hadn't been for the cold wind and the thick carpet of snow on the ground, it could have been summer.

"Looks like clear skies," Anna said to Elsa. She stood beside her sister in the sled. They were lined up alongside the four other teams at the starting line. A crowd of villagers had gathered to watch the Arendelle Cup begin. The towns-people murmured with excitement as the teams prepared to race.

Anna drew off one of her mittens. She licked her index finger and held it up, testing the air.

"What does that do?" Elsa whispered.

"I don't know," Anna replied, shrugging. "I've seen Kristoff do it before a journey. It looks important." She studied her finger carefully for a moment. Then she put her mitten back on.

"Did you learn anything?" asked Elsa.

"Yes," Anna answered. "I learned that

you shouldn't lick your finger and expose it to the cold."

Elsa laughed. "Better or worse than sticking your tongue to a frozen lamppost?"

"I just wanted to see what would happen!" Anna said. "And for the record, that lamppost looked *tasty*."

The girls giggled. Elsa thought it was nice to start the race on a light note. The other teams looked very serious, especially Team Weselton. Leopold was hunched over the reins, while Lutz frowned into the wind. Their two mules pawed the ground restlessly.

Nina and Naia from Eldora checked

the harness on their horses. The horses were a beautiful pair. One was gold and the other was chocolate brown. The winter wind blew through their manes. They snorted happily, ready for adventure.

Team Chatho looked focused. Their two yaks waited patiently at the starting line. They weren't the fastest animals, but the strong, shaggy creatures were very sure-footed in the mountains. The beasts lifted their heads to gaze across the landscape.

To the left of Anna and Elsa was Team Tikaani. Sivoy and Suqi held their six dogs in check, waiting for the start. The dogs were harnessed in pairs in front of

stood at attention with her ears pointed forward.

"Are we ready?" Elsa asked, gripping the reins.

Anna checked the bundle of supplies strapped to the back of the sled. "Ready," she answered.

"What about you, Sven? Ready?" asked Elsa.

The reindeer struck the ground with his front hooves, eager to race.

"I'll take that as a yes," Elsa said.

It was officially time for the race to start. The five teams looked expectantly at Kristoff. The ice harvester had been chosen to announce the start. He stood to the

left of the starting line, holding a green flag in the air.

"On your marks, get set, GO!" Kristoff shouted, waving the flag.

All five teams leaped forward—some faster than others. They thundered across the snowy plains. The villagers cheered them on. Elsa could hear the roar of the crowd over the drumming of hoofbeats.

The teams barreled along the opening straightaway. The wide path cut across a clearing. The trail stretched for miles, leading toward mountains and the frozen lake. On the first day, the race traveled across flat land. Everyone wanted to make good time before heading into the mountains on Day Two.

"Come on, Sven!" Elsa called encouragingly. She glanced over her shoulder at the two teams behind them. Chatho was moving slowly but steadily with their yaks. Eldora, on the other hand, was gaining gradually. Their fleet-footed horses charged closer.

"Faster, Elsa!" Anna shouted.

Elsa studied the two teams in front of them. Team Tikaani had pulled out into an early lead. The sled dogs ran perfectly in sync with one another, paws padding swiftly over the snow. Suqi held the reins and urged the dogs to go faster. But they needed little urging. They were born to run.

Straight ahead, Elsa heard Team

Weselton shouting commands. The mules clopped forward at a brisk pace.

"We can take them, Elsa!" Anna whispered. "They're not that far ahead of us."

Elsa gauged the distance. She realized that Anna was right.

"Hup, hup!" Elsa called to Sven.

Sven dashed forward, increasing his pace. The reindeer had a lot of energy. It was the beginning of the race, and he was happy to run. Within moments, he closed the gap with Team Weselton.

Lutz noticed that Team Arendelle was right on their heels. He tapped Leopold on the shoulder and whispered a warning. Leopold handed the reins to Lutz. He leaned down over the side of the sled and scooped up an armload of snow.

"What's Leopold doing?" Anna asked.

Elsa shrugged. She concentrated on pulling alongside Team Weselton. But before she could, Leopold dropped the snow right into their path! Sven trampled the soft snow, sending up a cloud of powdery frost. Elsa and Anna couldn't see a thing!

Elsa considered using her powers to clear away the frost. But she decided against it. She'd promised herself not to use her powers during the race. It wouldn't be fair to the other teams. Besides, she and Anna wanted to win without magic.

Seconds later, the cloud of snow settled. When they looked up, Team Weselton

had vanished. They could still see Team Tikaani in the distance. But Leopold and Lutz were suddenly out of sight.

"Where could they have gone?" Anna asked.

"Maybe they sprinted farther ahead?" Elsa answered uncertainly.

Anna shielded her eyes from the sun with a hand. She scanned the snowy plain.

"That was some trick!" she said.

It was Elsa's turn to smile mysteriously.

"What is it?" asked Anna.

"Well, they never would've pulled that trick if they didn't think we could beat them," Elsa explained.

"Oh," Anna said, catching on. "So we're not as inexperienced as they thought."

Elsa nodded. "We just qualified as competition," she said.

*

At sunset, Anna and Elsa made camp near a grove of snow-covered trees. They were exhausted and exhilarated at the same time. The first day of the race was over. They weren't the first team to reach the checkpoint at the foot of the mountains, but they weren't the last, either. They were proud of the day's accomplishments.

The sisters untied their camping supplies from the sled. They'd learned a lot about camping to prepare for the race. Kristoff had shown them how to pitch a tent and build a fire. He'd also shown them how to properly brush Sven's fur.

Anna tended the reindeer, while Elsa knelt to start a fire. Soon the camp chores were done. The girls sat side by side on a log next to the fire.

"Tomorrow's the mountains," Anna said, pointing to the tall snowcapped peaks.

Elsa rose and walked over to Sven. She

pulled a map from the reindeer's pack.

"I've been thinking about our route," she said to Anna. Elsa unfolded the map and handed it to her sister. "We should take Ragnor's Pass. It's higher in the mountains and it'll take more work to climb, but it's more direct."

"Let's do it," Anna said, studying the map.

"In that case, we'll need to get a good night's sleep," Elsa told her.

"Sven's one step ahead of you," Anna replied. The reindeer was snoring lightly on his feet.

Elsa laughed. She was just about to sit down again when a cold, wet nose touched her palm.

"Kaya!" Elsa gasped, surprised. The dog had padded silently into the camp. Kaya panted happily. She nudged Elsa's hand until it settled between her ears.

"I think she wants you to pet her," Anna said, smiling.

Elsa did, scratching the dog's head. "Sivoy and Suqi must be camped nearby," she said.

"Do your owners know you're here?" Elsa asked the dog. She had a feeling Kaya had sneaked away again. But Elsa didn't have the heart to send her back. The dog was so sweet.

Anna reached over to pet her, too.

Moments later, Sivoy emerged at the

edge of the camp. Elsa noticed him and waved hello.

"There you are!" Sivoy said, spotting Kaya. The dog lowered her head. She knew she was in trouble. Kaya slunk away from Anna and Elsa. She loped over to Sivoy's side. "I'm sorry if she caused any trouble," he said.

"She's no trouble at all," Elsa said. In fact, she admired the dog. Kaya was an independent spirit—not unlike her sister, Anna.

"She seems to like visiting you," Sivoy said.

"Well, who wouldn't?" Anna asked, joking.

Sivoy laughed. "How was Day One of the Arendelle Cup?" he asked them.

"Great!" Anna replied.

"But tiring," Elsa added.

"Any tips for first-timers?" asked Anna.

"Nothing you don't already know," he answered lightly. "But I guess just remember that while racing can be fun, it isn't everything. Some things are more important."

Sivoy thanked Anna and Elsa for looking after his dog. Then he set off with Kaya, heading for his camp.

"That's good advice," Elsa said.

"The best," Anna replied, nodding in agreement.

Chapter 4

Anna and Elsa woke the next morning ready to race. They quickly packed up their camp and hitched Sven to his harness. Soon, they were winding their way up into the mountains.

Elsa felt confident in her decision to take Ragnor's Pass. It was more difficult to climb but definitely more direct. It led straight through the snowy peaks instead of skirting the base of the mountains.

The trouble with Ragnor's Pass was that it was slow going. The trail was steep and slippery in places. Sometimes even sturdy Sven lost his footing. When Team Arendelle hit one particularly icy patch, Elsa and Anna climbed out of the sled.

"This is intense, Elsa!" Anna exclaimed. "It feels like we're going to slide all the way back down the mountain!"

"I think it's best if we walk for a bit," Elsa said. "We can lead Sven by his bridle and help him find his footing."

As Elsa and Anna walked alongside Sven, Team Chatho approached. Tenzin

and Tashi guided their yak-drawn sled up the steep slope. When they saw the sisters walking, they stopped.

"Is everything okay?" Tashi asked.

"Yes," Elsa answered. "It's just a little slippery up here."

"You two don't seem to be having any trouble," Anna pointed out.

"Our yaks were raised in the mountains," Tenzin said. "They're very steady on their feet."

"Can we offer you a hand?" asked Tashi.

Elsa and Anna exchanged a look. It was a nice offer, but the sisters were determined to make it on their own. Elsa politely declined.

Team Chatho wished them well and continued along the trail. They were bound to make good time with their nimble yaks.

"Do you think the other teams chose this route, too?" Anna asked.

"I'm not sure," Elsa said. "I guess it depends on how well their sled teams can handle the slope."

Sven nickered confidently.

"Of course *you* can handle it, Sven!" Anna replied. "But some of the other teams might not be as lucky."

Luck held for Elsa, Anna, and Sven as they continued their climb. Ragnor's Pass was steep, but it was also beautiful. The

higher they climbed, the more they could see of Arendelle below. Snow-covered fields stretched out toward the horizon. Tiny cottages dotted the landscape. In the distance, they could just make out the castle's tall turrets.

"We're a long way from home," Anna said.

"So are the other teams," Elsa replied. "They're even farther from home than we are."

*

Later, Anna and Elsa rounded a bend in the pass and came upon Team Eldora. Nina and Naia were pulled over on the side of the trail. One of their horses was lying on his side. Naia took a heavy blanket from her supply pack and spread it over the horse.

"What happened?" Anna asked. She and Elsa walked over to the cousins.

"One of our horses is sick," Naia explained.

"Oh, no!" Elsa said, concerned.

"He got into our plant samples," said Nina. She and Naia had been collecting plants along the trail. They showed the sisters a sprig of sturdy evergreen. It had a waxy leaf with pointed ends.

"Helvig's holly," Anna said.

"That's right," Naia replied. "It doesn't

grow in Eldora, so we thought we'd take a cutting home to study."

"Unfortunately, Goldie thought it looked tasty," Nina said. "We found him munching on it this morning. It gave him a stomachache."

Elsa looked at the golden horse, his head hanging low. He whinnied softly. Naia leaned down to rub his neck.

"Helvig's holly isn't good for horses," Anna said. "But I think I know something that can help."

"Kai's Sneezewort tea!" Elsa said, remembering. Kai was Anna and Elsa's royal handler. He had known them since they were children.

"He made it for me every time I ate something that looked tasty . . . but wasn't good for me," Anna explained sheepishly.

"Like lampposts," said Elsa.

"The tea didn't help with that one," Anna admitted.

"Do you think this tea can help our horse?" asked Nina.

"Yes," Anna answered. "Only, I don't think we have any Sneezewort."

Naia looked thoughtful for a moment. "Wait! Is the stem long and kind of hairy with sharp leaves?"

"Yes," Anna said.

Naia and Nina looked at one another hopefully.

"I think we picked a cluster of that yesterday!" Naia said. She untied a purple sack from the back of their sled and rummaged through it. "Is this it?" she asked, showing a plant to Anna.

Anna sniffed the hairy vine and immediately sneezed. "Yup, that's Sneezewort, all right," she said.

"If you like, we can show you how to make the tea," Elsa told them. "We've seen Kai do it many times."

"But it'll slow you down in the race," Nina pointed out.

"That's okay," Anna said with a smile. "Some things are more important than racing."

Chapter 5

As Elsa and Anna made camp that night, they thought back on the afternoon. They had spent several hours with Team Eldora. First, Anna had shown them how to make Kai's Sneezewort tea. Then they'd stayed to help nurse Goldie back to health.

By nightfall, Goldie was up on his hooves again. The two teams reached the checkpoint tied for last place. But Anna and Elsa weren't worried. They had all of next day to catch up. Besides, it was worth stopping to help out new friends.

By the time Elsa and Anna finished eating dinner, it was snowing gently. Anna snuggled deep into her heavy coat by the fire. All of a sudden, Sven began to fidget. The usually calm reindeer stamped and snorted.

"What is it, Sven?" Elsa asked. She knew Sven couldn't talk. But he had other ways of communicating.

Sven's nostrils twitched. He pawed the ground restlessly.

"What do you think he means, Anna?" Elsa said.

"I don't know," Anna replied, shrugging.

"But he's definitely trying to tell us something."

Elsa scratched her chin, considering. Kristoff usually knew what Sven was thinking. He often talked for Sven in a made-up voice. But Kristoff wasn't here now. "Could he be hungry?" Elsa asked.

"But we just gave him dinner!" Anna pointed out.

Elsa looked directly at Sven. She mimed eating, lifting an imaginary spoon to her mouth.

The reindeer snorted and shook his head.

"Well, food's out," Anna said. "How about water?"

Sven shook his head again. Then he looked up at the mountain peaks. He whinnied nervously.

"Maybe he misses Kristoff?" Anna suggested.

Sven gave an indignant snort.

"So much for that," Elsa said. She watched the reindeer closely. He swiveled

64

his ears toward the left, listening carefully. After a moment, he tilted his head, angling his antlers toward the mountaintops.

"What could he be saying?" Elsa asked. "Something about the mountains?"

"We've been in the mountains for an entire day!" Anna responded. "And he wants to tell us now?"

The reindeer paced back and forth beside the fire. He seemed to be worried. Moments later, he stopped in front of Anna and Elsa. Sven took a deep breath. Then he exhaled, making a loud rumbling sound right in Anna's face.

"Blech, reindeer breath!" Anna exclaimed, scrunching up her nose.

"Sven, that wasn't very polite!" Elsa said.

The reindeer didn't look at all apologetic. He was trying to tell them something important. His breath misted in the cold air.

"That noise," said Elsa. "What do you think he meant?"

"It sounded kind of like snoring," Anna replied. Suddenly, she slapped a hand to her forehead. "That's it, Elsa! He's trying to tell us you snore too loud!"

"What? I do *not* snore!" Elsa protested.

"Do too! You have no idea what it's like sharing a tent with you," Anna teased lightheartedly. "You huff and puff and grumble like Oaken's ice engine!"

"There is no way that I snore!" Elsa insisted.

"Why? Because you're a queen?" Anna asked, joking.

"I'm sure *some* queens snore. But this one does not!" Elsa told her.

"But how would you know? You're always sleeping when it happens," Anna pointed out.

"Uh, excuse us," said a voice. "Are we interrupting something?"

Anna and Elsa stopped their playful arguing. They looked up and saw Suqi and Sivoy walking toward them, Kaya following at their heels. This time the mischievous dog had brought her owners with her.

Elsa brushed her hands against her skirt, somewhat embarrassed. "No," she replied. "My sister and I were just having a minor disagreement."

"It wasn't really a disagreement. I was right and she was wrong," Anna explained.

Kaya put an end to the sisters' friendly bickering. She trotted over to Elsa and barked happily in greeting.

"Looks like Kaya's taking your side," Suqi said to Elsa.

Elsa and Anna invited Team Tikaani to sit beside their fire. Once they were seated, Suqi asked, "This might seem like an odd question, but has your reindeer been acting strangely tonight?"

Anna sat up straight. "As a matter of

fact, yes, he has," she answered.

"It's like he's trying to tell us something," Elsa told them.

Suqi looked at her brother. He nodded.

"Why? What's going on?" Anna asked.

"After we set up camp tonight, we noticed that our dogs were anxious," Suqi said. "They usually settle right down to sleep after a long day—well, except for Kaya." Kaya's ears quirked at the mention of her name. She placed her paws on Elsa's lap, begging to be petted. Elsa rubbed her gently.

"We decided to investigate," Sivoy explained. "Suqi and I patrolled the area around our camp."

The brother-and-sister team had

discovered a few interesting facts. First, that they were traveling on the leeward side of the mountain—the side protected from the wind. Next, that the snowflakes falling from the sky were needle-shaped instead of star-shaped. And lastly, they'd seen snow plumes.

"Snow plumes?" Elsa asked.

"Look," Sivoy said, pointing. Anna and Elsa looked in the direction of Sivoy's finger. He was pointing to one of the tallest mountain peaks. There, in the distance, white wisps of snow spiraled from the summit. They billowed outward like smoke.

"It's beautiful," Elsa said.

"But dangerous," Suqi replied. "All of those things are signs of an avalanche."

Elsa knew a lot about snow, but she didn't know that. "Is that what you were trying to show us, Sven?" she asked.

Sven nodded vigorously.

"Smart reindeer," Sivoy said.

Sven puffed out his chest proudly.

"What should we do?" Elsa asked worriedly.

"The good thing about avalanches is that if you know they're coming, you can avoid them," Suqi said.

She and Sivoy had scouted the area. They'd found another trail that led to the other side of the mountain. It was a little

out of the way, but much safer than staying on Ragnor's Pass. The snow in the pass was unstable.

"We can show you to the safe trail tomorrow morning," Sivoy said.

"Thank you," Anna replied. "That's kind of you. Should we warn the other teams, too?"

"We already did," Suqi answered.

Elsa and Anna were relieved. Thanks to Team Tikaani, they could steer clear of danger. The plan was for all of the teams to meet early tomorrow. Suqi and Sivoy would show everyone to the new path. They could start down the safe trail together.

"But don't worry," Sivoy said. "Once we're safely out of the mountains, there'll be plenty of time left for friendly competition."

"We look forward to a race to the finish," Anna told him, shaking hands.

Team Tikaani stood up to leave. Kaya sat and gave Elsa's hand a lick. Then she padded off behind her owners.

Chapter 6

"How did you sleep?" Elsa asked the next morning. She and Anna trudged through the fresh layer of snow on the ground. Ice crystals crunched under their boots with each step. It had stopped snowing only an hour ago. The few trees along the trail were covered in ice.

"Pretty well," Anna replied. "Your snoring woke me just once."

"For the last time, I don't snore!" Elsa said. She swatted Anna playfully on the shoulder.

Anna raised a skeptical eyebrow. "You heard her last night, right, Sven?" she asked the reindeer.

Sven looked away innocently. Instead of jumping into the exchange, he focused on pulling the sled. They were on their way to meet Suqi, Sivoy, and the others.

A few minutes later, Elsa saw the teams waiting on the path up ahead. They were standing at a fork in the road. Sivoy and Suqi were deep in conversation. Elsa and Anna stopped beside them. They noticed that Team Tikaani looked worried.

"Is something wrong?" Anna asked.

"Everyone's here except the team from Weselton," Suqi explained.

"Maybe they're running late," Elsa said.

"That's what we thought," Suqi replied. "Until Tashi found the tracks."

Tashi and Tenzin had discovered hoof-prints leading down the left fork.

"They look like mule tracks," Tashi said.

"Team Weselton is the only one with mules," Tenzin pointed out.

"So they left before us?" Anna said.

"They did," Sivoy answered. "Only, they went down the left path."

Elsa looked at the trail where it split in two. There was an old signpost in the

middle of the fork. The sign pointing to the left read RAGNOR'S PASS. The sign pointing to the right read INGRID'S LEAP.

"Ingrid's Leap is the safe path. It'll lead us to the windward side of the mountain," Suqi explained. "But it looks like Team Weselton stayed on Ragnor's Pass anyway."

"They'll get caught in the avalanche!" Elsa gasped.

Suqi nodded anxiously.

"We have to go after them and convince them to turn back!" Anna exclaimed.

"What about the race?" asked Naia. "It's the final day."

The team members looked at one another. Naia had a point. They'd all

trained very hard for the Arendelle Cup. Whoever stopped to rescue Team Weselton would finish in last place!

Elsa thought about it. Leopold and Lutz hadn't been very friendly. They'd bragged about being the best team. They'd even thrown snow into her and Anna's path. Still, she couldn't let them walk into an avalanche! Like Sivoy had said, some things were more important than winning.

Elsa glanced at her sister. She knew Anna felt the same way. After a moment, Elsa spoke. "The race doesn't matter," she said. "Not when someone could be hurt."

"Maybe we should all go," Sivoy suggested.

"That's a good idea," said Tashi. "We can all look out for each other and make sure Leopold and Lutz are safe."

Nina and Naia nodded in agreement. If everyone went, they would all make the same detour. It was a fair solution.

The four teams climbed into their sleds. They guided their animals to the left fork, following the mule tracks. Team Tikaani took the lead, followed by Arendelle, Chatho, and Eldora. One by one, they made their way down Ragnor's Pass.

Chapter 7

Elsa, Anna, and the others hurried along the pass. Midway through the mountains, the trail reached its peak. Then it wound downhill. On either side of the icy path stood steep slopes covered in snow.

"I hope we find Team Weselton soon," Anna said, guiding the sled around a bend.

"Me too," Elsa replied. She stared up at the snowy slopes, shielding her eyes from the sun. Was it her imagination, or did the snow seem to vibrate with each hoof-beat? "Slow down, Anna," Elsa said softly.

Anna obeyed, slowing Sven to a trot. The other teams noticed and slowed down too. Soon everyone stopped and gathered in the middle of the trail.

"What's going on?" asked Tenzin.

"I'm worried about those slopes," Elsa explained. "I think they're about to give way."

Nina and Naia squinted up at the mountains. "I don't see anything," Nina said.

"Me either," Tashi agreed.

"I know," Elsa said. "But something's wrong. I can feel it."

Team Tikaani gazed carefully at Elsa. They knew that the Queen of Arendelle had a special sense about snow. She could move it, shape it, and conjure it from thin air. Maybe she didn't have the ability to predict what it would do. But if Elsa thought something was wrong, they wanted to listen.

"What do you think we should do?" Naia asked Elsa.

"We need to go slowly and be careful," Elsa answered. "Any sudden movement could cause the snow to slide."

"That sounds reasonable," Tashi said.

"There's nothing wrong with being careful," Nina responded. Slowly, she picked up her reins and turned Eldora's sled. The horses stepped lightly, ready to continue on the trail. But just then, the ground rumbled dangerously.

Startled, everyone looked up at the icy slopes. The snow trembled and a giant sheet of ice broke loose! It slid rapidly down the mountain, gathering snow and momentum. The avalanche tumbled toward the pass, crushing trees in its path!

"Oh, no!" Elsa gasped.

She looked around her. All the teams were scrambling for cover. But there was no shelter to be found. Elsa knew what she had to do.

As the snow barreled toward them, she raised her arms. Elsa closed her eyes and concentrated. Her fingers spiraled through the air. The rolling mounds of snow were almost on top of them! But Elsa kept her cool and opened her eyes.

Palms out, she pushed her hands through the air in front of her. She transformed the sliding snow into a solid wall of ice. The teams quickly gathered behind the wall. But the snow kept tumbling! It threatened to spill over and bury them! Elsa spun and swiftly raised another wall on her right. The two walls shuddered as the snow pounded against them.

"I don't think it's going to hold, Elsa!" Anna shouted over the roar of the avalanche.

Elsa saw that Anna was right. Two walls weren't enough! She swirled her

fingers again and raised a third snow wall. Next, she added a fourth wall and a roof. Within seconds, she'd built a snow shelter, protecting the teams and their animals. Relieved, Anna and the others huddled close to Elsa. They were indeed thankful for her special power.

*

A few minutes later, the avalanche was over. The snow settled softly on the slopes and the rumbling stopped. The teams gazed about in wonder. Elsa's snow shelter was no ordinary place—the walls had crystallized into a beautiful ice chamber.

"This is incredible," Suqi said.

"I'll say," Sivoy agreed.

Tenzin and Tashi reached out to touch the glittering walls. The frozen crystals formed delicate, star-shaped patterns along the surface.

"We've always heard about your powers. But we never imagined they were so amazing!" Tashi exclaimed.

"It reminds me of something you'd see in Chatho's royal gallery," Tenzin said, pointing to the ice design. "Queen Elsa, you're an artist."

"Thank you," Elsa replied, blushing. "Only, I wasn't really thinking about art. I just wanted to keep us safe."

"You certainly saved us!" Naia said.

"We're really grateful," Nina told Elsa.

No one was prouder of Elsa than Anna. She hugged her sister tight. "Do you think it's safe to get out of here now?" Anna asked.

"Let's give it a try," Elsa answered. She used her magic to carve an ice door into a chamber wall. Anna grasped the door by

its frosty handle. She pulled it open, only to be met with a solid wall of snow!

"I guess that figures," Anna said. "We're buried."

Luckily, they had a snow queen on their side. Elsa wound her arms through the air and wiggled her fingers. The snow outside the chamber fell back from the door. It rippled away in huge white waves, like an ocean made of snow.

With the snow cleared, the teams emerged from the shelter, leading their animals out into the sunshine. Kaya barked happily. She was clearly thrilled to be under the open sky again.

Elsa, Anna, and the teams from

Tikaani, Chatho, and Eldora were eager to find Team Weselton. There was just one problem.

"The mule tracks—they're gone!" Tashi said.

Chapter 8

Each of the teams looked closely at the ground. The avalanche had changed everything! It covered the trail in mounds of snow, burying any tracks.

Elsa grew even more worried. If the avalanche had buried Team Weselton, there was no way to find them!

"What are we going to do?" she asked.

"I have an idea." Sivoy unhitched Kaya

from the sled team. The dog bounded free of the harness and sat. "Kaya has been trained to find people lost in the snow. Seek, Kaya!" he said firmly.

Kaya stood at attention. She tipped her nose into the air, scenting the wind. Her ears cocked forward. She tilted her head to the left and listened.

After a moment, Kaya's nose twitched. She padded forward, sniffing the ground in front of her.

"It looks like Kaya's on to something," Anna said. The dog crept forward slowly at first. But after a few yards, she broke into a trot.

"She's definitely found a scent," Suqi told them.

The teams piled into their sleds. They followed Kaya as she made her way over the uneven trail. The snow was very deep in some places but shallow in others. Kaya picked her way cautiously along the frozen path.

Suddenly, a tremor rippled through the ground. Elsa braced herself for another avalanche. But the snow on the mountain slopes didn't budge. Instead, the icy path in front of Kaya cracked and split apart! An enormous hole opened in the middle of the trail.

Kaya yelped, lost her footing, and tumbled into the hole!

"Kaya!" Suqi and Sivoy cried urgently. They were riding right behind her. They tried to stop, but the ground under their sled gave way. Team Tikaani pitched head-long into the hole!

Elsa's eyes widened in alarm. She pulled back hard on the reins. Sven dug

his hooves into the snow. He managed to stop just inches from the hole's edge.

"Oh, no!" Team Eldora shouted as they pulled up beside Elsa and Anna. Team Chatho was the last to rein in their animals. They skidded to a stop just behind Nina and Naia.

Anna and Elsa stepped cautiously out of their sled. They crept to the edge of the hole and peered down. Elsa studied the hole in front of her. It was actually pretty narrow—more of a crevice than a pit. Luckily, it didn't look more than twenty feet deep.

"Is everyone okay?" Anna called.

Sivoy and Suqi climbed to their feet.

They dusted the snow from their parkas and checked their dogs. Fortunately, no one was hurt. Even Kaya was unscratched.

"We're all right!" Suqi told them.

The other teams breathed a sigh of relief.

"Great! Now we just have to figure out how to get you out of there!" Anna turned to Elsa. "Do you think we can pull them up?"

"How?" Elsa asked.

"Well, I know we've got enough rope in our supplies. We could lower it down and haul them to the surface," Anna explained.

"It's two people, six dogs, and a sled

full of supplies. Won't that be heavy?"
Elsa asked.

"Maybe Sven could pull the rope,"
Anna responded.

The reindeer nodded eagerly. He was
ready for any challenge.

"Sven's pretty hearty, but it seems like
a lot," Elsa replied.

"What if we help?" asked Nina. "We
could harness your reindeer to our horses."

"And your horses to our yaks," Tenzin
told Nina.

"That should be more than enough
strength to hoist Team Tikaani up," Naia
said.

"Brilliant!" Anna said brightly. She

leaped into motion, unhitching Sven from the sled. The other teams did the same. Tashi and Tenzin made a new harness out of everyone's reins. They hitched all the animals together with Team Eldora's help.

Elsa took the rope from her supply pack. She knotted one end around the harness and lowered the other end into the crevice. Suqi caught the end of the rope and tied it to the sled. She climbed in with Sivoy and the dogs. It was a tight fit.

"Ready?" Elsa called from above.

"Ready," Sivoy replied.

Anna gave the signal to Sven. The reindeer was hitched to the front of the team, followed by the horses and the yaks. Sven lowered his antlers and began to pull. The

other animals joined him. Together, they lurched forward, lifting Team Tikaani's sled.

"Heave-ho!" Anna said.

The team of animals took another steady step. Inch by inch, they crept forward along the snowy surface.

"Keep going!" Tashi called.

Team Tikaani's sled rose higher and higher. Soon it was nearly level with Elsa. She stood at the rim of the crevice, ready to lend a hand.

"Almost there!" Naia said.

Moments later, the sled slid over the edge. Elsa and Tenzin leaned forward to give Team Tikaani a hand. At last, they arrived safely on the surface.

"Thanks for the rescue!" Sivoy said.

"Don't thank us, thank them," Elsa replied, pointing to the team of animals.

"Absolutely," Sivoy replied. He retrieved a supply pack from his sled and pulled out treats. There was grass for the yaks, apples for the horses, and a carrot for Sven.

"How did you know Sven liked carrots?" Elsa asked.

"We have plenty of reindeer back home in Tikaani," Sivoy answered, smiling.

Chapter 9

Even though Team Tikaani had been rescued, there was no time to celebrate. Everyone was still on the hunt for Team Weselton. Kaya picked up the scent again. She trotted quietly along the trail, alert for any signs of the missing team.

A short while later, Kaya padded to a stop. She turned in a circle and sat down, tail thumping eagerly.

"This must be the place," Suqi said.

They had come almost to the end of Ragnor's Pass. The path wasn't as steep anymore. Most of the ground here was flat. The mountain slopes faded into the distance.

Suqi and Sivoy climbed quickly out of their sled. They rushed over to Kaya. If Team Weselton was buried here, there was no time to lose!

The other teams raced to join them.

"Do you hear that?" Anna asked.

"I do," Elsa said slowly. There was a faint popping sound. It sounded almost like wood creaking.

"Where is it coming from?" Naia asked.

"It sounds like it's beneath us," Tashi answered.

"Maybe it's Team Weselton," Nina said.

Everyone leaped into action at once. Each of the teams pulled shovels from its supply packs. They began to shovel frantically—except for Elsa.

"I think I have a better idea," Elsa said.

She motioned for the other teams to stand back. Elsa raised her arms. She traced her fingers through the air. Soon the snow in front of her rippled and collected into heaping mounds. Elsa used her powers to lift the mounds of snow. It was much faster than shoveling!

The other teams looked on in wonder.

This was the third time Elsa had used her powers today, but it was still incredible to them. She scooped the snow from the ground and guided it through the air without even moving.

After a moment, Anna said, "Look!"

There, covered in a solid layer of ice, was the bottom of a wooden sled. The wood creaked under the weight of all the ice.

"It's that popping sound!" Tenzin said.

"It must be Team Weselton!" Suqi exclaimed. "Or at least their sled."

"Just the sled?" Tashi asked.

"Maybe they're hiding underneath," Naia answered. "To protect themselves from the avalanche!"

Just then, the ground rippled and rumbled.

"Easy, Elsa," Anna told her sister.

"That's not me," Elsa replied. "It's another tremor."

"The snow is still unstable," Sivoy explained.

"Let's rescue Team Weselton and get out of here!" Nina said.

Elsa stared at the bottom of the sled frozen in ice. "With the snow so unstable, I'm afraid my powers will cause another avalanche."

"But how can we get them out?" Naia asked.

Tenzin and Tashi exchanged a look. "Maybe we can help," said Tashi. She reached into her pocket and took out a mallet and a chisel. "Tenzin and I are sculptors."

"That's brilliant!" Anna said, catching on. "You can chisel the ice away."

Elsa agreed. "It might take longer, but it'll be much gentler."

Tenzin and Tashi climbed down to the frozen sled. They used their tools to chip away at the ice little by little. Both were careful not to hammer too hard. Any sudden movement might cause another avalanche.

After several minutes, the sled slipped free of the ice. Tenzin and Tashi lifted it. Team Weselton was huddled underneath. Even the mules had managed to squeeze in with them.

"Thank goodness you found us!" Lutz said. "We were riding along Ragnor's Pass when the avalanche hit."

"There was nowhere to take cover, so we ducked under the sled," Leopold explained. "It's a good thing you got here when you did. We were running out of air."

"We're glad you're okay," Tenzin said.

Elsa, Anna, and the other teams helped Team Weselton climb up to the surface.

"How in the world did you clear away all the snow?" Leopold asked.

"Queen Elsa did that," Suqi said.

Leopold turned to face Elsa. "I owe you an apology," he said.

"Me too," Lutz chimed in.

"We were so busy trying to win, we didn't care about having you as friends," Leopold admitted.

"And there's something else," Lutz said sheepishly. "We cheated. We took a short-cut on the first day."

"We're very sorry," Leopold said.

Elsa frowned. She didn't like the way Team Weselton had acted. But she could tell they were truly sorry.

"I accept your apology," Elsa said. "But you should tell the others you're sorry, too. Cheating affects everyone in the race."

"Can you forgive us?" Lutz asked the other teams. "Not only for cheating, but also for taking the wrong trail."

"We put you all in danger when we decided to stay on the pass. I hope we can make it up to you somehow," said Leopold.

All the teams accepted, to the relief of Lutz and Leopold.

Chapter 10

"Bad news," Tashi said. She and Tenzin had just finished inspecting Team Weselton's sled. "It's broken."

"Is there any way to repair it?" Leopold asked.

"We don't have the tools," Tenzin replied, shaking his head.

"That's okay," Lutz said. "We'll have

the mules tow it back and we'll walk beside them."

"That'll take forever! You'll finish in last place for sure," Naia said.

Team Weselton shrugged. "We deserve last place," Leopold said glumly.

"Nobody deserves a broken sled," Anna said.

"Especially not a friend," Elsa added.

"Are we friends?" Leopold asked. "I thought after everything that happened—"

"Of course we're friends," Anna said.

Leopold and Lutz beamed from ear to ear.

"So how about a lift, friends?" Elsa asked Team Weselton. "We'll help tow

you from here to the finish."

"We can't let you do that," Lutz said. "It's your first race. You'll finish in last place with us."

"We'll do it, then," Suqi offered. "We don't mind. We've won twice in a row."

"But you were going to make it three! The fans will be disappointed," Nina said. "Naia and I can tow them in."

"Nonsense," said Tashi. "Our yaks are used to towing heavy loads. We'll do it."

"Wow," said Lutz. "I've never seen so many people eager to finish last."

"Wait a minute," Elsa said, considering. "If we all tow you in, we'll all finish together."

"You mean we'd tie for last place?" asked Anna.

"No," Elsa said. "No one would be in front of us. We'd tie for *first* place!"

Everyone smiled.

"Elsa, I like the way you think," Anna said with a wink.

Later that day, all of Arendelle gathered to see the results of the Arendelle Cup. Kristoff stood fidgeting at the finish line. Olaf bounced eagerly next to him. They were both rooting for Elsa, Anna, and Sven. So they were completely surprised to see all five teams cross the finish at the same time!

It was an unusual sight—so unusual that Kristoff wasn't sure who to name the winner. He waved the checkered flag, signaling the end of the race.

"And the winner is . . ." Kristoff didn't know what to say next.

"EVERYONE!" Olaf shouted.

For the first time in the history of the Arendelle Cup, all five teams had won.

*

The next morning, Elsa and Anna said goodbye to each of the teams. Tenzin and Tashi were the first to leave. They promised to give Anna and Elsa's regards to Queen Colisa. Next, Nina and Naia said farewell. They were thrilled to return to Eldora with the recipe for Kai's Sneezewort tea. Leopold and Lutz were the third team to depart. They were leaving Arendelle with something even better than a win—new friends.

Team Tikaani was the last to leave. Sivoy and Suqi hugged Anna and Elsa goodbye. Kaya barked happily at Anna. Then she tucked her head under Elsa's hand and demanded to be scratched. Elsa rubbed her gently behind the ears. Kaya licked her face in farewell.

As Team Tikaani set out across the snowy plains, Anna and Elsa walked back into the castle. Anna noticed that her sister looked a little sad.

"What's wrong, Elsa?" Anna asked.

"The tough thing about making friends is that you always miss them when they have to go home," Elsa replied.

"I know," said Anna. "But we're lucky.

We're friends who *share* a home."

"We're not just friends," Elsa said. "We're sisters . . . and Arendelle Cup cochampions!"

© Jenn Carvin Photography

Erica David has written more than forty books and comics for young readers, including Marvel Adventures *Spider-Man: The Sinister Six.* She graduated from Princeton University and is an MFA candidate at the Writer's Foundry in Brooklyn. She has always had an interest in all things magical, fantastic, and frozen, which has led her to work for Nickelodeon, Marvel, and an ice cream parlor, respectively. She resides sometimes in Philadelphia and sometimes in New York, with a canine familiar named Skylar.